Diary
of a
Noob Steve

....

Book 1

MC Steve

Contents

Sunday
Hundreds of Blocks High

I always said it would never happen to me. But it did. I lost everything in the fire. I had no choice but to come here to Stone Towers so I could re-craft my life and start a new adventure.

I'm not the only one. I'm not the first. I was one of the last to arrive tonight.

For months now, all over this world, there have been fires. Mysterious Fires, they are calling them. They are calling them that because no one knows where they are coming from. One minute my house was fine. I was about to go to sleep. Then all of a sudden everything was on fire. There was nothing I could do to stop it.

I took another step forward. It was all behind me now. I knew I had to focus on what was ahead instead of on what had already happened.

Dog nudged my hand with her nose as we approached the city.

"What is it, girl?" I asked. She looked up, so I did the same. I couldn't see the top of the wall from where we were standing. "Wow! That wall has to be hundreds of blocks high!"

Made of stone bricks, it looked sturdy. Unbreakable.

"Two hundred and thirty-eight, to be exact," one of the guards said as Dog and I finally reached the open gate. "You know the rules?"

"Uh, yes!"

Dog whimpered. The guard glared down at me.

"Uh, no."

Another guard appeared. He looked like he wanted to hurt me. "You! Explain the rules to the refugee as you're escorting him down to his...cell."

"My cell?" Dog backed away a little. "You're putting me in prison?"

"Those are the rules," the guard said, motioning for me to follow him. "Don't worry. There will be plenty of time for me to explain."

Monday
The Rules

"The rules," said the guard, "are as follows."

He recited them to me as we slowly rode in mine carts toward where I assumed the prison must be.

Each refugee that arrives at the gates of Stone Towers must go through a twenty-four-hour waiting period. They have to spend this time in a cell. I was about to ask why, but then he explained further, and it made more sense.

At the end of that waiting period each refugee is required to go through a strict set of evaluations. A test, basically. They judge your skills and see what you are best at. Then they place you in the district that best fits your skills.

There are six possible districts they could put you in. They could put you in the crafting district, the fishing district, the brewing district, the farming district, the mining district, or—my favorite—the defense district.

I knew that was where I'd get sent. I fought mobs all through the night to get here with almost full health. I knew what I was doing.

"So what happens after that?" I asked the guard. We were still moving slowly along the rails. I didn't see any sign of a prison anywhere.

"You work," the guard answered.

"For how long?"

The guard smiled. "Forever."

I shrugged. "All right. Works for me."

All of a sudden the rails our mine carts were riding on took a steep drop downward. We were going fast then. I could hear Dog barking from the mine cart behind me. It was over pretty fast. We rolled to where the tracks stopped. We all got out, and the guard led us down a dark tunnel. Too dark. I thought I might have heard a mob. Nothing happened.

He stopped so suddenly I almost ran into him. Then a door to my left opened, letting in some torch light.

"Your cell," the guard said, and I stepped inside.

There was a bed in the corner. The floor and walls were made of bedrock. I realized pretty quickly that the light wasn't coming from torches at all.

The ceiling was made of glass. Above that single layer of glass sat lava.

The cell was small enough that if you broke one of those glass blocks, there would be no way to avoid the lava as it came down.

"Your tools, please," the guard said. "Your armor, too."

"My tools? My armor?" I protested. "But...ah, let me guess. Rules?"

11

"You got it," the guard said, still smiling.

So I dropped all my tools: my diamond sword and pickax and shovel. I dropped all my armor, too. He picked it up, put on my diamond helmet, and laughed.

"Will I ever get them back?" I asked hopefully.

He didn't answer. He just walked out of the room and closed the door.

So that's it. Trapped until tomorrow. The only way out? Death by lava.

All I have now is what's left in my inventory: some food to share with Dog, my diary, and some random objects I picked up off the ground on my way here. They took my tools. Everything in here's made of bedrock, so you can't even dig out with your hands.

I've laid everything out in my cell, and it doesn't look like much. There's nothing to do except write. And sleep.

This is going to be a very long twenty-four hours.

Tuesday
The Test

wo things: one, I'm not dead. And two, I have my own house now. But I'm getting ahead of myself. Let me back up.

Once it got dark I fell asleep in an instant. There was a loud knock on the door as soon as I opened my eyes again.

"Who is it?" I asked, Maybe, I hoped, it was someone coming to rescue me.

"Security," barked an unfamiliar voice from the other side of the iron door. "Here to escort you to your evaluations."

The guard opened the door and gestured for me to follow him.

"Don't I get breakfast first?" I asked as I approached the doorway, but he didn't answer me. I motioned for Dog to follow us down the long, badly lit hallway. There were wide open spaces on the walls where torches should have been. Like someone forgot to place them.

The guard led us to a few mine carts, which led us back above ground and through a seemingly deserted part of the city. The guard that got me out of my cell rode in the cart in front of me, Dog rode in the cart behind me, and another guard rode in a cart behind her. We rode all the way to an open area covered in nothing but grass.

"Welcome," a man said as I stepped out of the mine cart. "Are you ready for your test?"

"Uh." I thought about it. "Can I study first?"

"No," the man said. "This way."

The man led me to the middle of the field, where there were a bunch of trees standing in a row in front of me. That was it.

A group of men stood behind me. Dog stayed off to the side, whimpering.

"It's okay, girl," I said. "Don't worry."

The man stood beside me, looking bored.

"You will gather wood," he explained, "craft a weapon, find a diamond, harvest as many crops as you can, and defeat a designated enemy. You have twenty minutes. Depending on your performance, you will be placed in a territory of our choosing."

"Can I give you my top three?" I asked.

"Ready," the man said, ignoring me. "Set. Craft!"

And so, with all the objectives he had given me, I did what I had to do to make sure I would never have to go back to that cell with the lava ceiling ever again.

I punched down a few trees, built a crafting table and crafted a pickax and a bow with arrows. I harvested all the wheat in sight. As quickly as I could I dug and dug until I found a diamond. I tossed it toward them as I looked around for my target and saw a single cow standing in the distance. And another. And another.

"Which one?" I asked, frantic. I was running out of time.

"All of them," the man said. So I fired arrows, one after the other as fast as I could.

I sent an arrow through the last cow, who did not survive the hit.

I turned back to face the judges, still holding the bow in my hand.

I had finished with just enough time to spare.

"Did I win?" I asked. Dog barked.

The man spent a lot of time writing in a book. Then he showed the book to the other judges, who only nodded. The man turned back to me.

"Based on our evaluations, you will be placed in a lot in the Stone Towers farming territory," the man said. "That is where you will live and work in exchange for food, shelter, and permission to stay inside our walls."

"But I—" I started to protest, but the man kept talking as if I had not said anything. I was good at more than just farming and I knew it.

"Our head farmer will escort you to your new home," he said.

"This way," the head farmer said, and he, Dog, and I walked in the opposite direction, toward my new home.

Wednesday
The Farmhouse

All I have to say is for a small farm out in the middle of nowhere, inside a city surrounded by a giant wall, this place is...TOTALLY AWESOME!

By the time the head farmer and Dog and I finally made it to our destination, it was getting dark out. So he led me into the house where Dog and I would be staying. Except for a bed, the place was completely empty. And small, too.

"Where's all the furniture?" I asked him as I looked around the room.

"You have all you need," the head farmer answered. "Oh, wait. Almost forgot."

In front of me he dropped three wooden tools: a shovel, a hoe, and an ax.

"Shovel's for digging," he instructed. "Hoe's for planting. Ax is for chopping."

"Wood?"

"Cows," he corrected. "Pigs. Sheep. Just follow the signs."

He turned to leave through the open door, but I stopped him with another question. "Signs? What kinds of signs?"

He gestured for me to follow him outside and pointed to the spot above the door. "New signs will be up every morning with instructions telling you what your task is for the day. Someone will come by every few days with new tools. For when yours break."

I just shrugged. I can craft my own when that happens. "Who puts the signs there?"

With a shrug, he turned and left the same way we had come.

"Oh, and one more thing," he said, turning to face me again. "Stay inside once it gets dark. Not much light out there. Don't want to run into any unfriendly mobs."

"Yeah. Got it. Sure." I planned on crafting a sword later, just in case.

Since it was already late, I decided to sleep. I woke up to the sun in my eyes through the east window, and that is when I decided to start looking around to see everything I couldn't see when we got here the night before.

I spent the whole morning exploring. This place has cows and sheep and chickens and pigs and horses, all fenced in. It has a ton of trees. And it also has blocks and blocks of crops, wheat and potatoes and carrots and even sugarcane along a river that runs through the whole thing. There's a bridge running across the river and, beyond that, a forest.

Since it's my first day, I don't have any tasks yet. I check all the crops and harvest and replant a few. I pick up all the chicken eggs on the ground just in case I'll need them for something later.

Thursday
Language of the Stone Towers People

I guess you could say my second full day on the farm was...interesting.

I was instructed to build a new pen for the horses that someone would be bringing to the farm next week. They laid all the pieces out on the ground in front of my door, and all I had to do was build it based on their instructions.

It was supposed to be a square, fifteen blocks each direction with a gate exactly in the center. I figured it didn't need to be that big, so I made it ten squares on every side with a gate in the corner instead. There are already a lot of friendly mobs around; I'm not really sure what this place needs horses for. But I was bored, and placing the fence pieces on the ground didn't take very long. So I took it all apart and did it again. And again. And again.

By the time I got bored with that, almost the whole day was gone.

It was getting dark. But I'm not afraid of the dark. The head farmer had told me not to stay outside after the sun went down, but his warning didn't make any sense. If any mobs spawned around, I knew I could take them. I had fought much worse on my way to the city. Anything I would find out in the fields I knew I could handle.

I was not expecting to make a new friend in the darkness.

After exploring for a little while I started chopping down trees. For what purpose, I did not know; it just gave me something to do. I heard a few mobs in the distance once it got really dark and the moon came up, but nothing too threatening.

Then I heard a different noise. Something close. Something familiar.

Enderman.

Endermen are easy to handle when you know what you are doing. As long as you do not look at them or touch them, you can win.

For some reason none of those rules made sense this time around.

My first instinct, when I turned around and saw the Enderman, was to grab for my wooden ax, which I had been using to collect more wood. I know that if you ignore endermen, they won't hurt you. There was just something about this one that made me feel nervous.

I charged forward. Since the Enderman wasn't facing me, I figured I might be able to catch it off guard. It turned around at the last second.

A strange noise stopped me in my tracks.

"Wait! Wait!" a voice called out, and I gripped tight to my ax but didn't swing it. The enderman teleported around me a few times, then stopped at the top of a hill a short distance away. "Don't hit me!"

"That was *you*?" I asked the Enderman, almost dropping my ax on the ground. "Since when can endermen *talk*?"

"They can't!" the Enderman answered. Its voice was high-pitched and sort of sounded like it was speaking from underwater. "Except for me. I can. I'm the only enderman who can. Which is why they...banished me."

The Enderman hung its head like it was sad.

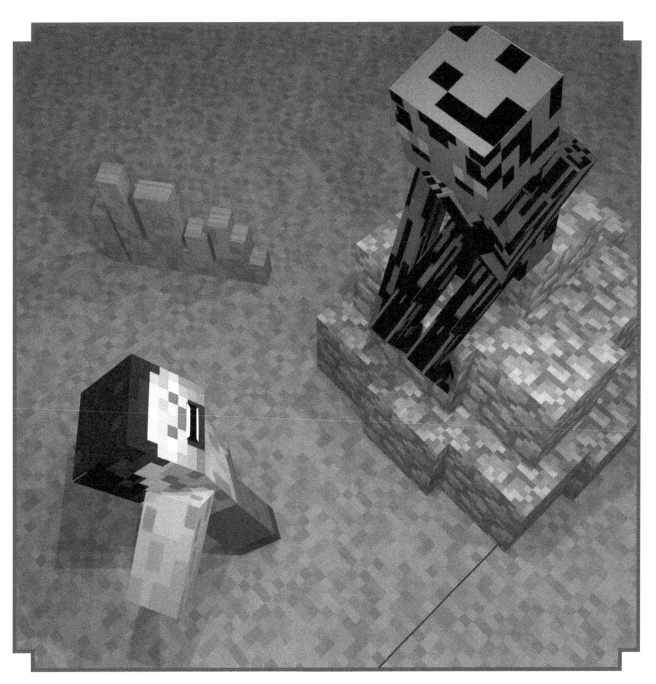

"Banished you?" I asked. "From The End?"

"Mm-hmm," the Enderman hummed. "I'm the only one who can speak the language of the Stone Towers people. I see it as a gift, a special talent. Others see it as a curse. Something I should be...ashamed of."

"I think it's kinda cool," I said, not afraid anymore. Not that I was ever afraid in the first place, I mean. I'm not scared of endermen. "I'm Steve."

"We don't have names where I come from," the Enderman said. "But it's a pleasure to meet you, Steve. It's getting dark. You'd better go."

"Oh, you're right," I said, looking around. I hadn't noticed how dark it had gotten since we had first started talking. "I'll see ya later!"

I never thought I would become friends with an enderman. Then again, I suppose stranger things have happened.

Friday
The General's Daughter

Well, things have gotten worse. Much worse.

The good news is I don't have to go back to the bedrock and lava cell they put me in when I first got here. The bad news is I'm under house arrest.

That's right. Not even a week in Stone Towers, and I'm already in trouble.

Being under house arrest means that I'm not allowed to set foot outside my front door. If I do...well, I'm not really sure.

It all started when I woke up this morning and went outside. As the head farmer had said, there was a new sign posted on the front door telling me the job I needed to do that day. I needed to harvest wheat, carrots, and potatoes; replant everything I harvested; and then take what I harvested into town so it could be distributed at the market.

I did exactly as I was told, as any good citizen-to-be would do. I harvested all the wheat, carrots, and potatoes in my field (I only ate one potato, I swear) and replanted everything so it could start growing again. Then Dog and I set off into town.

23

It was a much shorter walk into town than it had seemed walking the other direction with the head farmer before. There were a lot of people around, and I could tell they were all from different districts. The miners were all wearing iron helmets, even though they weren't underground where mobs might be. All the crafters were carrying wood planks and stone bricks in their hands. Other farmers, like me, were carrying food.

"Excuse me," I tried to ask someone. "Where do I deliver my food?"

I asked one person, and they ignored me. The next three people I asked ignored me, too. There I was, standing in the middle of town with a bunch of food and no one to give it to, when I saw a girl walking ahead of me. She disappeared between two buildings. Dog kept looking in her direction, so I decided to follow her. Maybe *she* would talk to me.

"Hello?" I said as I rounded the corner. "Hey, do you know where—"

But I never got to finish asking her that question, because the moment I spoke, something crawled out of the darkness straight toward her.

A spider.

All I had on me were my wooden shovel, hoe, and ax. But I couldn't just let that spider attack her. She stood there, frozen, not moving, not trying to defend herself or even turn and run away. There was only one thing I could think to do: attack it before it attacked her.

So I took my shovel and ran toward the spider. The girl screamed. I wasn't sure what was going to happen. I had no idea how many hits it was going to take to kill it, or how many it might take to kill me first.

But the spider must have fallen from a high place before it started crawling toward us, because I only hit it once, and it was gone.

"Are you okay?" the girl asked me, out of breath like she'd just run all the way across the world. "Did it hurt you?"

"Nah," I said, trying to play it cool like I hadn't been scared. I mean, I hadn't been scared. Not really. "But you should be more careful. If I hadn't been here..."

"I know," she said. "So, uh...you're new here, right? One of the refugees?"

"Uh...yeah," I answered. "Hey, do you know where I go to deliver my food?"

"Yeah, of course, I can show you, if you want."

"Awesome."

We stepped out of the shadows and started moving toward the direction in which I had come, but we didn't make it very far.

Dog started barking, and at first I couldn't figure out why.

"Stop!" a voice called. "You're under arrest!"

25

Saturday
Potion of Invisibility

Under arrest?" I looked around. Everyone around me was backing away. What seemed like hundreds of armor-wearing soldiers were closing in. "What did I do?"

"Interference with Stone Towers defense protocol," said a man with green eyes, black hair, and dark skin. He wore armor made of iron, like the rest of the soldiers.

"What does that even mean?" I asked.

"Nobody," the man said as he got closer to me, "fights off mobs except members of the Stone Towers defense district *only*."

"But she almost got attacked!" I protested. "I saved her life!"

"Nobody," he said again, inches away from my face, "fights off mobs. Especially refugees who are not part of the Stone Towers defense district."

"All right, all right," I said, backing away slowly. "I'm new here. Didn't know. I'll keep that in mind for next time."

"We'll see about that," the man said. Dog barked again and kept barking that time. "Do you know who I am, refugee?"

26

I held up a hand. "First of all, the name's Steve. Steve the Noob. You can just call me Steve. Second of all—"

"I asked you a question, refugee!" the guy yelled, and Dog stopped barking.

"Don't yell at him!" the girl who I'd saved not two minutes ago defended.

"That's enough, Jillian," he said sternly, turning toward her. "You shouldn't have been anywhere near that alley."

She tried to protest again, but he held up a hand, silencing her. When he turned back to me he didn't look quite as mad as he had before Jillian interrupted him. "I am the General. I am the head of the defense district here in Stone Towers. Normally, that would give me the authority to throw you right back in detainment. Permanently."

"But you're not going to," I tried. "Right?"

The General sighed. He was not happy. "You broke the rules, kid. Big time. But you also saved my daughter's life."

"Jillian is your daughter?"

He nodded. "So, as you can probably guess, I'm facing a dilemma here. I would—should—punish you. You're a refugee. You don't have rights. But if it weren't for you, Jillian could have been seriously hurt. Or worse."

"Come on, Dad, go easy on him," Jillian urged. I smiled at her. The General groaned.

"Five days," he said. "In five days you will stand a fair trial, in high court, just like any other Stone Towers citizen. That is your reward."

"So...what's my punishment?" I had to ask.

28

"Until your trial," he answered, "you will be put under house arrest. You will be escorted back to where you have been assigned to live, and you will not be allowed to leave. You will stay there until one of my soldiers comes to get you and brings you back into town."

"So you're telling me I'm not even allowed to farm?"

"You will not set even a toe outside your front door. Do you understand?"

"How will you know if I leave my house or not?" I asked. Not to be rude or anything. I just wanted to know.

The General gave some kind of hand signal to his soldiers. In unison they all took something from their pockets and drank it. Then they disappeared.

"Potion of invisibility," the General said, grinning. "We'll be watching you."

As if the guy didn't creep me out enough already. I'm shuddering just thinking about it.

A group of soldiers marched Dog and me back to the farmhouse, made sure we went inside, and then disappeared. For all I know there could be one standing just outside the door, making sure I don't break the rules again.

There's not much to do around here, being stuck inside and all. It's not even close to being dark enough to sleep. What to do, what to do...

Sunday
Underground Cave

Hello? Steve? Are you down there?"

I never expected Jillian to find me down here. Then again, I never expected to dig out an entire underground cave beneath a farmhouse while under house arrest for saving the General's daughter, either.

See, what had happened was I got bored. So I took some wood from the floor of the house and made a crafting table. And then I made myself a shovel and a pickax. And by that point I figured there really wasn't anything stopping me from seeing how far I could dig down. What else was there to do?

"Jillian?" I asked, poking my head around a corner. I was about to start digging in a new direction, just to pass the time. "What are you doing down here?"

"Looking for you," she answered.

"But why?"

"Because I wanted to thank you in person for saving me in the square. And tell you I'm sorry that it got you into so much trouble."

"Ah, it's okay," I said. "It was worth it."

"Where are you digging to?" she asked, looking around the cave. "And how did you dig all this without any tools?"

"I crafted my own tools," I said. "You know, like this." I crafted a stack of sticks from some wood planks left in my pocket to demonstrate.

"Right," she said, sounding nervous. "Well, now that I'm down here I might as well do some exploring with you. If that's okay."

"Sure," I said. "Let's dig this way."

"What was that?" Jillian asked a little while later, and I turned around just in time to see a skeleton coming around the corner. Just as it was about to fire an arrow at her I jumped in front of her and took the hit. The battle was tough, but I won it.

"You saved me...again," she said.

"All in a day's work."

We walked in the opposite direction as if the skeleton had never been there at all.

Monday
Mob Trivia

Jillian was quiet for a long time after the skeleton attack. I figured it was because she was scared of more mobs showing up.

"You don't have to be afraid," I told her. "I put more torches down. We're safe."

"It's not that," she said with a sigh. "You wouldn't understand."

"Try me," I challenged, switching to my stone shovel to continue digging through a patch of dirt in front of us.

"Well…" She thought about it as I dug and we continued moving forward down the tunnel. "There's a reason I didn't defend myself against that skeleton back there. It's just that, well…I'm the General's daughter."

"What does that matter?" I asked. "It means you should be good at fighting, right?"

"Not exactly," she said. "In Stone Towers, sons and daughters of government officials aren't allowed to learn any skills. No crafting. No cooking. No farming or fishing or anything at all. Especially not anything about tools or weapons."

"Bummer," I said, only half concentrating on my digging. "Not to sound rude or anything, but...what CAN you do?"

"Lots of things," she promised. "Read, mostly."

"Books?"

"Tons of books. Not any books about skills, but books about why fishing and farming are good for the city. Stuff like that. But my favorite books to read are books about mobs."

"There are books about mobs?"

"Tons. I've read them all. I know everything there is to know about mobs, even the stuff most people don't know. Go on. Ask me anything. Bet you can't stump me."

"Wanna bet?" I stopped digging for a second so I could think of a question that only I would know the answer to. How much can a person really learn from a book, anyway? "How close does a skeleton have to be before it starts firing arrows at you?"

"Eight blocks."

I thought harder. "How much more powerful is the explosion from a charged creeper than an explosion from a regular creeper?"

"Twice as powerful."

I was sure she wouldn't get the third one. I saved the hardest for last. "What do you call a group of endermen?"

"A haunting."

"You DO know everything there is to know!" I exclaimed. "That's amazing!"

"I told you so," she said. "Don't stop now. We could be near a cave."

"But I haven't eaten anything in two days," I argued.

"Didn't you bring any food with you when you decided to come down here?"

"I never thought I'd get this far."

"Ugh!" Jillian threw her hands in the air. "You better be glad I have a whole stack of carrots with me. If it weren't for me, you'd starve."

"Why do you have a whole stack of carrots?"

"No reason."

Tuesday
The Secret

After we ate our midnight snack of carrots with a side of carrots and some carrots to go with them, I started digging again, with my pickax this time, and she told me more about all the things she had learned about mobs as we kept moving through the massive tunnel.

I can't believe how much she knows. Much more than me, and I thought I knew it all. I guess that's what happens when you are only allowed to do one thing your whole life. You may not be good at a whole bunch of different things, but you're super good at that one thing. I am almost jealous.

"Do you think we should turn back?" Jillian asked.

"What for?" I asked. "We've got to be getting close to something soon. A mine shaft, maybe. Maybe even a dungeon!"

"It's just...your trial is coming up pretty soon. And sooner or later someone is going to come looking for me. What if they find the hole you dug? You could be in huge trouble."

"No way," I argued. "I'm under house arrest. If I walk out the front door of my house, I'll go to jail and stay there forever."

"And?"

36

"Haven't walked out the front door of my house, have I?"

She rolled her eyes.

"Fine," I said, turning back to the wall. "Just a few more blocks this way, then we'll go back. Dog probably misses me anyway."

The next block that I hit did not have another block behind it. We had finally dug into another cave from the one I had started.

"See?" I said, turning to look at her. "Aren't you glad I didn't stop?"

"Be careful," she said as I removed another block and then another, opening up the space so we could walk through it.

This was not your ordinary cave.

"Wait..." Jillian looked around, and so did I. This was not a cave at all, but a tunnel lined every fourth block or so with torches on either side of it. It was three blocks wide and three blocks high and seemed to go infinitely in two directions. "What...is this?"

"Part of something the miners dug up, maybe?" I wondered.

"I didn't think they dug anywhere near here," she said. "Besides, they use TNT. This looks like it was dug out by hand, block by block."

"Let's see where it goes," I urged. "Come on."

"Wait." She hesitated. "Which way should we go?"

37

"You go right and I go left?"

She shook her head. "We don't know where this tunnel goes in either direction. If there are any mobs…"

"You're right." I looked down the tunnel in one direction, then the other. They looked exactly identical, all stone blocks with evenly spaced torches. "Let's go right."

"Why right?"

"I dunno. Let's just see where it leads."

"Okay," Jillian said. "Uh...I'll follow you."

So we set off down the tunnel. It felt like we walked for days before we came to something other than stone walls and torches. The tunnel turned left at a right angle.

"Hold on," Jillian said, grabbing my arm. "Do you hear that?"

"Hear what?" I asked.

"Voices. Listen."

So I listened. She was right. In the distance we could hear voices coming from around the corner, down what was probably another long hallway. These weren't any mobs, though. They were people.

"They're coming toward us," Jillian said, suddenly panicked again. "What do we do? There's nowhere to hide..."

"Wait."

The voices stopped, and I heard the sound of two stone blocks breaking not too far away. Slowly I peeked around the corner and saw a hole in one of the walls of another long hallway two blocks wide, just wide enough to walk through.

there." I pointed, and together we moved toward it. As we approached I could see that this was not another long tunnel. There was no stone on either side. It was a room.

Quickly I turned and ran back around the corner where we had come from. I used my pickax to dig a nine-square hole in the wall, which gave us a full view of what was happening on the other side of it.

What we saw I would not have believed if I would not have seen it for myself.

There was a giant room made of all stone, filled with people. At the very front of the room there was what looked like the entrance to another tunnel, but it was only a few blocks deep. It had torches placed on every block inside it, and before it stood a man who looked like he had killed an ender dragon and lived to tell the tale.

He was not smiling. I just hoped he wouldn't see us.

"Attention!" He called out suddenly, and both Jillian and I hid behind either side of the opening, just in case. Reluctantly, we both peered inside the room. "If anyone has any updates to share, speak now."

"I, sir."

"You may speak," the man said.

"We seem to be out of cake, sir."

Voices mumbled in protest all throughout the room. "No more cake?"

40

"Forget about the cake!" the man in front of the torches yelled. The room quieted down again, fast. "Does anyone have any IMPORTANT updates to share with the group? Ah, yes, you. This better be good."

A different man stood up and cleared his throat.

"More refugees are set to arrive later tonight, sir," he said.

"Good, good. Have the fires been put out?"

"Yes, but everything is destroyed. As he requested."

"Excellent." He smiled. "When he told me his plan, I thought it would never work. Setting fires to settlements, on purpose? Drawing the refugees to Stone Towers? It didn't make sense to me. But the more I thought about it, the more I realized how right he was."

"What do you mean?" someone else asked.

"Tell me, ladies and gents, could you craft a diamond sword right now if I gave you the materials and a crafting table?" Everyone shook their heads. "Could you plant and harvest crops? Fish? Mine for coal?"

Everyone shook their heads again. I looked over at Jillian, who looked angry.

"Our citizens don't know how to work in more than one district of Stone Towers, if even one at all. That means not enough work is being done. The best solution seems to be...well, having the refugees do it for us."

"Gah, this is so boring," I whispered.

"Sshh." Jillian put a finger to her lips.

"What happens when there are no more settlements left to burn down?" someone asked. "Will these refugees be enough?"

"Looks like they're the only choice we have," said the guy in charge. "They may be trash, but they know how to work, now don't they?"

This guy was totally ruining my day. I mean, first he tried to bore me to death, and then he called me trash. I had to do something. Then I remembered I still had the chicken eggs left in my inventory from my first day on the farm.

"Steve, what are you doing??!!"

But it was too late. I had already thrown a chicken egg around the corner. Great aim, too. It sailed down the hallway and through the meeting room, just barely missing the head of the guy who was standing between the wall of torches.

"Who did that?" he said, looking around. A few people in the room were laughing. "That is not funny! This is serious. You! Figure out where that chicken egg came from, NOW."

"Uh-oh," I said, and Jillian and I hid around the corner again.

"Did you really have to throw a chicken egg at his head?" Jillian whispered.

"I was bored! And he called me trash!"

"Wait, listen," she said, silencing me. "Did you hear that?"

We both completely tuned out the voices in the meeting room and listened. In the distance we heard an enderman teleport...

It popped up right beside us, looked at me, and nodded.

Jillian gasped, but I shook my head. "It's okay. That one's on our side."

It took off down the hallway, toward the meeting room.

She frowned. "You're friends with an enderman?"

"Long story."

The Enderman stopped a short distance away from the meeting, made a noise, and proceeded to teleport around the meeting a few times.

The people in the room did not remain calm. Quite the opposite, actually.

"Enderman! RUN!!"

"Don't look at it!"

"Light! We need more light!!!"

"Wow," the Enderman said in its smooth, watery voice as the group scattered and scrambled in the opposite direction. "These guys sure don't like mobs, huh?"

Jillian looked like she was about to pass out. "It can...talk?"

"I told you it was a long story," I reminded her. To the Enderman, I said, "Hey, thanks. You really saved us just now."

"We're not all bad, you know," the Enderman said, sounding offended. "We just don't like to be looked at."

"Why is that, anyway?" Jillian asked, having fully recovered from her surprise— probably out of curiosity, since she knew all there was to know, and more, about mobs.

She must have startled the Enderman, though, because it teleported away before it could open its mouth to answer her. It did not come back.

Wednesday

The Argument

Cover the hole," Jillian said as soon as we reached the surface again.

"What? Why?"

"Just do it! Before anyone sees or follows us up here!"

"All right, all right, sheesh." I put the wood planks all back in place where they had been before. It looked like we had never gone underground at all. "Happy?"

She didn't answer at first. She went to all the windows and looked out, probably to see if anyone was watching. I guess she forgot about the potion of invisibility.

"Steve, what are we going to do?" she finally asked me.

I crafted and placed a chest against the wall and started dumping cobblestone into it. "What do you mean?"

"I mean, we just discovered a super secret plot that's affecting the whole world! We know that the Mysterious Fires are being started ON PURPOSE! We have to tell someone!"

"Why?"

"Because! We're the only ones who know! It's up to us to stop this!"

"Up to us?" I finished dumping the cobblestone into the chest and crossed the room to where Dog sat quietly in the corner. "You mean up to you."

"I'm not the only one who was there—"

"It isn't my responsibility, Jillian."

"What do you mean, it isn't your responsibility?" I never thought I would ever see Jillian mad. Everything changes about a person when they're mad. "You were there. You heard the same stuff I did. You can't just pretend you didn't."

"I'm not FROM here, Jillian!" I was mad, too, and I felt bad about that, but I needed her to listen to me. "Sorry, but I don't owe you or anyone else in Stone Towers anything. And besides, for all we know, the MAYOR could be involved. I'm already under house arrest. I can't afford to get into any more trouble."

"Yes, you can," she said calmly.

"No, I can't."

"Yes, you CAN, Steve." She walked to the window and looked outside again. It was the middle of the day. She was right; someone would probably come looking for her soon. "You saved me. Twice. You might not think that's a big deal, but here, in Stone Towers, it is.

"You may have gotten in trouble. But now we know why. It's because it's the government's fault that not enough people here know skills. If they see that refugees like you can do everything they can't, they might want to start a revolution."

"What would be so bad about that?" I asked.

"That's exactly my point," she said, turning away from the window. "You're more skilled than anyone in Stone Towers. Even more skilled than my dad. If you wanted to, you could use those skills to stand up against the government. To save the world. You could be a hero."

"A hero?" I said. "I never thought about it like that."

"Will you help?" she asked, practically begging for me to say yes. "Please? I...I don't think I can do it without you."

I thought about it. "Ah, okay. What do I have to lose?"

Jillian cheered. Dog barked. I could have sworn I heard my enderman friend making a noise from somewhere deep beneath the house to let me know it approved.

Thursday
The Plan

I am going to write out our whole plan in detail before I forget any of it.

That's right; we came up with a plan.

Today, Jillian is going to sneak into her dad's office and find a list of all the refugees that have come here and which territories they are living in. She is going to try and find as many of them as she can, so that they can show up at the trial.

We are going to wait until the General is about to give me my punishment. And then one of the refugees is going to stand up and yell, as loud as he can, "Objection!"

This will make the General really mad. But that will be my chance to stand up and start telling him what has been going on behind his back.

"Your council is betraying you!" I will tell him. "Someone is telling them to start the fires! Don't you see?"

He won't, of course. He will never believe a refugee, or even his own daughter, for that matter.

So we will have to make him believe that his own men are turning on him, even within the walls of Stone Towers. It is the only way we will be able to get our point across.

Just outside the location where the trial will be taking place, Jillian and a few of the refugees she talks to today will start a fire in the middle of the square without anyone knowing so that the General thinks it was one of his men.

It is risky and dangerous. My favorite kind of adventure.

I just hope nothing goes wrong. This is our only chance.

We are the only ones who know that the Mysterious Fires are being started on purpose. It is up to us to tell the general.

My trial is tomorrow. Someone will come and get me early in the morning and take me and Dog into the city.

Before Jillian left I crafted a stone pickax and sword and gave them to her to hide for me. I am not allowed to bring anything with me to the trial. I will bring this diary and nothing else. But it will all be worth it.

Tomorrow everyone will find out the truth.

We are going to save the day.

Even if my home is destroyed and I can never go back to it, Jillian is right. A lot of people have been hurt by this evil plot, myself included. It's time someone pays for what they have done.

I hope they get put into those cells with lava in the ceiling. That will sure show them.

Friday
The Explosion

Things didn't exactly go as planned.

Do they ever?

The trial was all ready to start. I was standing in front of everyone, ready to accept whatever punishment the General was going to give me for fighting off a mob in the square (even though I saved Jillian's life in the process).

"You," the General said into his microphone in front of everyone, without calling me by name, "are in big trouble."

"But I saved Jillian's life," I argued. If I didn't know a refugee was going to disrupt this entire conversation, I probably would not have argued with him. But I wasn't afraid of him. I mean, not that I ever was. "That alley should have had better lighting."

"You are on trial for committing a crime!" the General responded. I had to hold my breath to keep from laughing. "Do not speak unless you are spoken to. Do you hear me?"

I decided not to answer him.

"I said, do you hear me, refugee?" he bellowed.

"What? Oh, sorry. I heard you."

"Good," he said, totally annoyed. "You know why we're here. I don't have to repeat myself. Fighting off mobs is not a refugee's work and is punishable by exile."

"Exile?" I repeated, a little bit more worried. I hadn't expected the punishment to be that severe. "But where?"

"That," the General said, smiling, "is for me to decide."

I looked back nervously at Jillian, who was standing by the door with a few refugees beside her. When she saw me she nodded once, and she and the refugees went out in the square to get ready.

I turned back to face the front. This was it. Now or never.

"Before we move on—" the General started to say.

Then it happened.

Something we had not planned at all.

"Creeper!" I heard someone in the crowd scream. A lot of people had showed up to watch me get punished. But no one had expected anything like what happened next.

"Creeper?" The General drew his sword. "Where?"

Jillian and the refugees came back, having heard the disruption.

"The entrance to the mine! There!"

We all turned. Right off the square was the mining entrance, where miners climbed into mine carts to take them down into the caves and bring them back up again.

At the mouth of that cave stood a creeper. But not just any ordinary creeper. Much, much worse.

"It's charged!" I shouted, running toward the General, who had started moving toward it. No matter what, I had to stop him.

"Its explosion is twice as powerful as any creeper you've ever seen!" Jillian warned, running toward us. "Don't!"

But it was too late. Even though everyone was already moving as fast as they could away from the entrance to the mine, I realized that the General held a flint and steel in his hand. He was going to make the creeper explode on command. Right inside the mine's entrance.

"Dad, no!" Jillian shouted just as the charged creeper detonated.

The entire ground shook. The noise was loud in my ears.

When we looked back at the entrance to the mine, it was destroyed. There was a big hole in the stone. No one moved. No one knew what to do.

"Somebody please tell me there weren't any miners working down there today," the General said to no one in particular.

As if on cue, my enderman friend teleported three blocks away from the General, causing him to scream and stumble back.

"They're trapped!" the Enderman said, and everyone started freaking out. "They won't be able to get out!"

People were scattering all over the place. I ran toward the microphone. "Hold on, hold on! It's trying to tell us something!"

"The miners!" the Enderman said. "They're trapped down there."

"The explosion must have ruined the rails leading down there," the General said.

"Their tools are almost broken," the Enderman continued. The General listened, even though you could tell he was terrified of the Enderman. "They're starving, and they don't have any food. They need help."

"And they can't dig themselves out," Jillian observed. "Or defend themselves."

"We'll send a team down," the General said, turning. "Men! Assemble!"

No one moved.

He cleared his throat. "Troops! Assemble NOW!"

One soldier stepped out of the crowd.

"Sir," he said. "We can't mine a path down there. We don't know how."

The General clenched his fists. "Does anyone in this town know how to mine blocks?"

I stepped forward. "I'll go."

"No one asked you, refugee," the General said.

"Let him," Jillian said, stepping forward. "He knows how to do everything. He'll be able to mine his way down there AND defend the miners. He can bring them back to safety."

"Absolutely not," the General said.

"Then who else will?" Jillian said, then stood up a little taller. "How about me?"

"Don't be ridiculous, Jillian."

"I'm not, Dad," she argued. "If no one else will go, I will."

"We'll both go," I said. "We have to. The Enderman is right. They need help."

"Hurry!" the Enderman said, teleporting away.

Without waiting for anyone else to give permission I took Jillian by the hand and leaped through the opening, taking her with me into the darkness. Dog followed close behind.

Saturday
The Game of Lava

On the way down I slipped off a stone and fell.

It was only four blocks to the ground, and it didn't hurt very much, but when I sat up I realized it was almost completely dark.

"Got any torches?" I asked Jillian.

"Nope."

"Me neither. Uh. This way. I think."

We started moving through a cave, listening carefully for mobs. I had my sword in hand and walked in front of her. We rounded a corner and saw light.

"There," she said, pointing.

"Wait." We both stopped. I took a few steps forward, and just then a skeleton fell from somewhere above, right in front of Jillian. She screamed, but it was already dead.

"Pick up that bow and those arrows," I told her.

"But I don't know how to shoot things!"

"I'll teach you," I said and kept walking toward the source of light. I guessed it had to be a bunch of torches the miners had put down. "But not now. They must have gone this way."

We walked toward the light. It turned out not to be torches at all but a river of lava flowing down. I turned to the left to see if I might be able to reach the top of the mountain.

"There they are!" Jillian said suddenly.

"Where?" I asked. I turned and took a step...and started falling.

"Steve!" she shouted. Then I heard an arrow coming toward me.

The arrow hit me, but it made me fly to the side, so I didn't fall into the lava. Startled, though, I ended up dropping both my sword and pickax into the river, never to be seen again.

"Nice aim," I said. I could hear a lot of mobs not too far off in the distance. It must have been night. The miners were trapped on the other side of the river with no way to get across or defend themselves against mobs.

We were all doomed.

Sunday

Battleground

What now?" I asked, feeling completely useless. "We can't get across. My tools are gone. I don't have any blocks in my inventory."

"But they do," Jillian said and turned to face them. "Can you hear me?"

"Save us! Please!" one of the miners called from the other side of the lava river.

"Listen to me," Jillian called. "You have cobblestone in your inventories! You're going to have to place it over the river so you can get across."

"They're coming!" Another miner came running toward the group. "They're coming!"

"Skeletons," I said, listening closely. "At least two of them."

"You're going to have to work together to fight them off!" Jillian said. "Use whatever tools you have left! Use your hands if you have to!"

"But we can't!" a different miner protested. "We don't know how to fight!"

"Listen to me," Jillian said again. "A skeleton won't start firing at you until it's eight blocks away. So get as close to the edge of the river as you can. Half of you, stand in front. When they get close, run toward them. Your diamond armor will protect you. The rest of you, come out from behind and start hitting them as many times in a row as you can!"

"But what if we can't take them all?"

"I have one arrow left," I said, holding the almost broken bow Jillian had picked up. "If I fire at one of them, it will get distracted. That's when you hit it."

"You can do this," Jillian said. "Into position! Hurry!"

The miners moved as close to the lava as they dared. The skeletons marched closer. As soon as I got one in sight, I aimed and fired the last arrow left over from the two Jillian had picked up after the skeleton had fallen in front of her.

"Missed," I said. "Oops."

"Look," Jillian said. As we watched, the miners did exactly as she had told them to do. Some of them ran in front and took a few arrows while the others charged and started hitting one of the skeletons. In no time at all it broke apart. Then the second one.

"You did it!" Jillian said. I threw the now-useless crossbow into the lava. "You did it!"

"Now we can get you out of here," I said.

"Wait," one of the miners said. "What's that?"

I stared off into the darkness of the cave beyond. A pair of purple eyes stared back at me before disappearing.

"A messenger," I said. "Going to tell your families you're on your way out of here."

Monday
Out of the Darkness

Together the miners built a bridge across the lava river and followed us back toward where we had come from. When we reached the spot I turned to face the group. Everyone was quiet.

"Is everyone okay?" I asked. I looked up to where you could see the sky; the sun was just starting to rise.

"We're okay," the head miner said, removing her helmet. "Thanks to you. You saved us."

"We're not out of the cave yet," I said. "Do you have any tools left at all?"

"Two stone pickaxes," she answered. "But they're almost broken."

She dropped them in front of me. "Good enough. Jillian, take this."

I dropped the extra pickax at her feet. "What for?" she wanted to know.

"You gotta help me dig a path back up to the surface," I said, walking toward the spot where we had dropped down from a few blocks up.

"But Steve, I can't," she said. "I don't..."

"Yes, you can," I said. "Come on. We have to get them out of here before more mobs show up. It's not light out yet."

She nodded. "Okay. Okay, I can do it."

So we did. We started digging a path up toward the former entrance so the miners could climb, block by block, up to the top. It took much longer than I thought it would, but Jillian started getting the hang of mining the blocks. The miners followed close behind us, clearly still afraid of being attacked by more mobs.

By the time we all made it out, the sun was high up in the sky. A crowd had gathered around the destroyed entrance, and they were waiting for us as we emerged. We let the miners out first, then Dog, Jillian, and I followed close behind.

We were all safe.

Everyone cheered.

"Thank you," the head miner said again as the noise died down. "If it wasn't for you..."

"You're welcome," Jillian said. "I'm glad you're safe."

"Yeah. Me too," I said.

"Jillian." We turned around as the head miner walked away, and the General was coming toward us, not looking happy at all. "How dare you disobey me."

"I didn't do anything wrong," she argued.

"I specifically told you not to go down there."

"And let those miners get hurt? They needed help!"

"It wasn't your job to save them," the General said. Jillian got really mad then.

"This is your fault!" Jillian exclaimed. "If it weren't for these stupid rules, if everyone in Stone Towers was allowed to learn any skills they wanted to, these miners never would have been in this much danger."

"I'm not arguing with you about this anymore," the General said. "We're going home."

It was then that Dog started to growl.

Tuesday
The Book

I had never seen Dog act that way around anything but mobs. And as far as I knew, there weren't any mobs around.

I should have known something was wrong. But I didn't.

"Dog, stop it," I scolded, but she kept barking at the General. "Dog! Stop!"

Instead of listening Dog growled louder, barked, and jumped toward the General as if she were going to attack him. Surprised, he fell backward onto the ground. A book lay next to him on the ground, glowing.

"What is that?" Jillian asked.

Before the General could react fast enough I picked up the book and opened it. "I don't believe this," I said out loud as people started gathering around us.

"What?" Jillian asked. "What's in there? Let me see." I handed her the book. "This... no. This can't be right."

"Jillian, it's not what you think," the General promised. But we both already knew he was not telling the truth.

"So this is how you did it," Jillian said, looking down at her father, waving the book around in the air. "This is how the Mysterious Fires were started. It wasn't the city council who wanted those refugees here. It was you."

The crowd around us gasped. The Mayor stepped forward.

"How could you do this to us?" he wanted to know. "How could you do this to me? I trusted you to protect this city, not poison it with lies!"

"I was just trying to do what was best for Stone Towers," the General argued. "Jillian is right: there aren't enough people with skills here."

"But this? This wasn't a solution!" The Mayor shook his head. "This was wrong. You've done something only a traitor would do."

"How dare you," the General said. "Me, a traitor? After all I've done to try and help?"

"There will be consequences," the Mayor said. "But not now. For now you will remain in the same cells you put all these refugees into. Tomorrow the council and I will decide what we are going to do with you."

A few guards took the General away in a mine cart. Jillian was quiet. So was Dog.

Wednesday
The Punishment

Everyone in Stone Towers showed up for the trial the next day, in the same space I was supposed to have mine the other day before that creeper showed up.

Everything was different this time. When it had been my trial, people were mad. They didn't like the fact that a refugee was being given a fair trial for committing a crime. This time everyone was shocked. Everyone expected a refugee to do terrible things. No one expected one of their own would do something much worse.

"General." The Mayor's voice, amplified by a microphone on the table in front of him. "Do you understand why you are here?"

The General nodded. "Yes, sir."

"Do you understand that you are on trial for a crime so disgraceful we are going to have to come up with a new punishment if you admit to it?"

The General nodded again. "I do."

I was just glad it wasn't me down there being punished. Even though I did feel bad for Jillian. She wanted to come watch this.

The Mayor cleared his throat.

"Do you admit to being responsible for starting the Mysterious Fires, destroying innocent people's homes and treating refugees badly?" the Mayor asked the General.

The man looked sad but tired. "Yes," he said.

"Do you understand why it was wrong?" the Mayor asked.

The General looked around. "Refugees are people, too," he said.

"And?" the Mayor said, waiting.

"And I never should have told anyone they couldn't learn skills outside of their district. Skills are for everyone to learn and use equally."

"Very good," the Mayor said. "Please give us a moment. The council and I must discuss the details of your punishment in private."

It was completely quiet. Not even Dog made a noise or wagged her tail. The Mayor and the council stood in a huddle, discussing things we could not hear. Eventually the huddle broke, and the Mayor stepped up to the microphone again.

"We have made our final decision," he said, and almost all at once everyone leaned forward to hear the news. "Exile."

"What?" He stood up.

"You have been banished, General," the Mayor said. People in the audience started to talk amongst themselves. "To the End. Temporarily. Maybe a few dozen hauntings of endermen can teach you how to have more respect for other beings."

"But..." He looked over to where Jillian and I sat. "My daughter..."

"I can take care of myself, Dad," Jillian said. "I promise."

The General agreed to the punishment. They are going to send him through the End portal tomorrow. Maybe then things will start to get back to normal around here. Which means it will be time for me to leave Stone Towers for good.

Thursday
The Portal

"Are you sure you want to do this?" I asked Jillian as we entered the dungeon.

"He's my dad, Steve," Jillian said in response. "He may have done some pretty bad things, but he's still my dad. I still love him, and I still want to say goodbye." She paused. "And, you know, this will probably be the last time I see him."

"Bummer," I said. Dog whimpered behind us. "But, uh…make it quick if you can. This place kind of creeps me out."

"Me too," she said. "He should be in here."

Two guards stepped aside to let us through. Behind a wall of iron bars stood the General, looking bored. When he saw us he came right up to the bars.

"Jillian," he said. "You didn't have to come here. I'm fine."

"I just came to say goodbye," she said. "You're strong. I know you'll be fine."

"It's time I learned my lesson," he said. "Maybe…maybe someday I'll be back."

72

"Time to go," one of the guards said. He got rid of the iron bars and made sure the General's hands were tied behind his back before leading him toward the End portal. Jillian, Dog, and I followed close behind.

When we got there, an enderman—my enderman friend—was waiting for us.

"W-what are YOU doing here?" the General asked nervously.

"I'm here to escort you to your destination," the Enderman said, being nice on purpose because she knew it scared him. "One moment, please. Stay."

"Look at you," I said. "All important, running errands for the Mayor."

"I was hoping I would run into you before we left," the Enderman said, turning away from the General, who glared at me from behind it. "I owe you a huge thanks, you know."

"What for? You were an important part of our team."

"But before I met you, I had no confidence!" the Enderman said. "Now I do. When I found those miners I knew I had to warn you. And when I saw they were safe I teleported back and let everybody know. They weren't even afraid of me. Now the Mayor has made me the official ambassador between Stone Towers and the End, and it's all thanks to you. You made me confident in my special skill. Now everyone back home respects me. They treat me like the leader I really am."

"That's great," I said. "Congratulations."

The General didn't like the fact that we were having such a pleasant conversation, making him wait to enter his worst nightmare.

"Are you done yammering yet?" he complained. "Let's just get this over with already…"

The Enderman turned to him, opened her mouth, and started shaking, the same way all endermen do when they're about ready to attack you.

"All right, all right, I'll wait!" the General said, backing away from us, his hands still tied behind his back. "Don't hurt me!"

"As I was saying," the Enderman said as she turned back to me, completely calm as if nothing had happened. "I would still be hiding out in that field all by myself if it weren't for you. I'll never forget you, Steve the Noob."

"Take care," I said with a wave. "Say hi to the Ender Dragon for me."

"Oh," the Enderman said as she floated up behind the General, just in front of the portal to the End. "We will."

Then they were gone. I turned around, surprised that Jillian was still there.

"Sorry about your dad," I said. "Hey. Maybe he'll learn to like it there."

"Yeah," she said. "Maybe you're right."

"Come on," I said. "Let's get to the party before they start without us."

"What party?"

"Come on," I urged. "You'll see."

Friday
The After Party

Everybody cheered as we walked toward the square.

I could tell Jillian was not comfortable with the whole thing. I guessed she wasn't used to being the center of attention. I didn't mind so much and made sure she kept walking next to me with her head held high.

"You earned this, Jillian," I reminded her as we got closer. "You helped save those miners. You're just as much of a hero as I am."

"You really think so?" she asked.

"Don't ask me," I said. "Just listen to them."

And she did. They kept cheering even after we had made it well into the square. There was a big bonfire in the middle and lights all around (probably to keep the mobs away, but it was still quite festive). There was food and music and lots of laughter. Even Dog seemed to be enjoying herself until the fireworks.

At one point Jillian and I lost sight of each other. As things started to wind down I went looking for her and almost walked right into the Mayor. He looked glad to see me,

"Well, Steve," he said, "other than throwing this party in your honor, I'm not sure of another way to thank you for all you've done for Stone Towers."

"Ah, it was nothing," I assured him. "Just doing what I do best."

"What's that?"

"Accidentally being in the right place at the right time."

He chuckled.

"I don't think anyone else would have had the guts to do what you and Jillian did for those miners," the Mayor said. "It has been quite a long time since I have seen anyone as skilled as you are."

"I try," I said, shrugging my shoulders. "For what it's worth, Stone Towers is full of great people, skilled or not. Even if somebody only has one skill, they can still make a difference in the world. Don't you think?"

"Hmm." He thought about that for a moment. "I suppose you are right. But I can't have any more of my council starting fires just so we can keep this place up and running. I'll have to pass a new law—one that lets everyone learn all the skills they want."

"That's a great idea," I said. "People like Jillian deserve to learn."

"Very true," he said.

We stood there in silence for a little while. I thought about doing another lap around the square to see if I could find Jillian, but he spoke again just as I was going to start walking.

"You know, Steve," the Mayor said, sounding thoughtful. "Now that the General is…occupied with other things, we're going to need someone to replace him in Stone Towers defense. Someone who is good at fighting off mobs and protecting our citizens." He paused. When I didn't say anything, he went on, "I would love it if you stayed. My people trust you. You're a true hero."

"I appreciate that," I said. "But I don't think that's the right path for me. Stone Towers is great and all, don't get me wrong. That wall is impressive."

"Thank you."

"But staying in one place too long…it might mean I wouldn't get to have many more adventures. I'm a nomad, don't you see? The whole world is my home."

"I understand," the Mayor said with a sigh. "At least wait until morning, though, okay? It's dangerous out there in the dark."

"Oh, I know," I said. "Fine. Just one more night."

I'll keep my word. I owe that to the Mayor. Tomorrow morning Dog and I will head out and leave this adventure behind us.

Saturday
The Next Adventure

It was almost sad, walking through town so early in the morning. There weren't any people around. I guess everyone was still tired from the party last night.

The same guard who brought me into Stone Towers that first night, who I learned last night is named Geoff, led me to the gate again. I was almost ready to walk through it, Dog walking not far behind me, when someone called my name.

"Steve!"

"Huh?" I turned around. "Did you say something, Geoff?"

"Wasn't me," he said, shrugging.

"Steve!" the voice called again. "Steve! Wait!"

"Jillian?" She ran up the steep incline toward the gate. By the time she finally got to me, she was completely out of breath. "What are you doing here?"

She took a moment to catch her breath before answering.

"I have something for you," she told me. "A goodbye present. A few, actually."

"Cool," I said. "I love presents."

She dropped a few stacks of items in front of me. Two stacks of carrots, and...

"I harvested them myself," she said excitedly. "From the ground!"

"That's great," I say, picking up the items. "I love carrots. And poisonous potatoes."

"Oh." She shrugged. "Oops. Sorry about that."

"It happens." I hesitated. "So...I guess this is goodbye."

"I guess so," she said. "I wish you could stay."

"I don't belong here, Jillian," I said. "You know that. There's so much I still haven't seen. This world is huge. I'd miss it all if I stayed here forever."

She nodded. "Just...promise you'll come back and visit, at least."

"Of course." Then an idea hit me like a skeleton's arrow. "You should come with me!"

"Steve..."

"You could learn all you need to learn out there," I encouraged her. "You'd love it. And without your dad..."

But she shook her head again. "I always thought maybe I would want to go on tons of adventures someday. But everything that's happened since you got here, well...I guess that was enough adventure for me to last a lifetime."

"Makes sense," I said. "Well, good luck learning all your skills. With that new law the Mayor passed, you'll be able to know it all in no time."

"I can't wait." She waved goodbye to me and to Dog. "I hope you find what you're looking for out there."

"Me too," I said, waving back. "Me too."

So Dog and I went on our way, off in the direction of the sun to find a place to build another tree house. Who knows what kinds of adventures are out there? We'll face them together, as good friends do.

Get YOUR Name
Listed on Our Website!

How would you like to be listed in the
Hall of Fame section of our website?

If that's a YES, then just leave a review for this book on Amazon
with your first name and first initial of your last name.
(Example: Derek P.)

Find Out How Steve Became A Zombie!

www.TheMCSteve.com

CPSIA information can be obtained
at www.ICGtesting.com
Printed in the USA
LVHW060714281020
670037LV00029B/179